Praise for *Roy of the Rovers*

"It has **everything that a football fan needs...** match day action, local club ri~~~~ ~~~~dern football politics, trials, crunching tack~~~~ ~~~~ ~~~~als It also has everythin~~~~ as they grow up. It is ~~~~ ~~~~ models, girls' involv~~~~ respect, mental well-being, g~~~~ education and aspiration." – *Books for Topics*

"Packs a lot of punch in its short and simple to read pages... **It captures the feel of playing and having a passion for football** at an early age very well. More than that it sets out the stall of the new Roy Race, his family background, his friends and enemies, where he lives and his work ethic." – *Comic Scene Magazine*

"**I give it 5,000,000 stars**! I recommend it to 9+ football fans but also non-football fans. I'm not a football fan but I still really enjoyed reading this book. Look out for the graphic novels and the rest of the series. Amazing!" – *The Book Brothers*

"**Football-lovers will love the description of on-pitch action** which is pacy yet satisfyingly detailed. This is a book that I am looking forward to putting on the shelves at school – I know already that it will be a popular title amongst our football-loving children
~~~~ ~~~~ch

First published 2020 by Rebellion Publishing Ltd,
Riverside House, Osney Mead, Oxford, OX2 0ES, UK

ISBN: 978 1 78108 826 5

10 9 8 7 6 5 4 3 2 1

A CIP catalogue record for this book is available
from the British Library.

Printed in Denmark

Creative Director and CEO: Jason Kingsley
Chief Technical Officer: Chris Kingsley
Head of Publishing: Ben Smith
Editor: Rob Power   Design: Sam Gretton   Cover image: Lisa Henke
Marketing: Bobby McGill

Follow us:

royoftheroversofficial   royoftheroversofficial   royoftherovers

www.royoftherovers.com   info@royoftherovers.com

ALSO IN THIS SERIES

For Helena Pielichaty, the Lily Parr of the children's book world.

ROCKY RACE'S ABILITY to predict the future had been improving in recent months.

It was weird, but it also made perfect sense. Since she'd started playing in a proper organised football team, she understood the game of football much better. So much so, she could imagine what was going to happen next, or even, the two or three things that might happen from any one moment in the game. And the more Rocky Race played the game at a high level, the more naturally that understanding came to her.

Rocky studied her captain Ffion Guthrie's

position on the pitch, as the ball came looping over the centre circle towards her. Rocky was so single-minded about the game it was like there was nothing else going on in the world – in her life – other than the trajectory of the ball. Football was an obsession for her. A passion.

In her state of 100% focus, Rocky foresaw the game's future once she took control of the ball.

Ffion would drift wide, finding space on the far touchline.

Rocky would play in a high ball, too high for Ffion to control with her feet or chest, so Ffion would rise above all the challengers from the surprised Hebden FC players, head it back to Rocky, who would now be unmarked in the centre circle. Then Ffion would sprint between two out-of-position defenders towards the goal, just as Rocky slid a perfectly-weighted pass in to her.

Sowerby Football Club were the best women's team in Melchester and the county beyond. This was thanks, in no small part, to the partnership of Ffion Guthrie and Rocky Race, their two star players.

Sowerby had enjoyed an astonishing season in which, coming from nothing, they'd risen to find themselves part of the football pyramid – a structure of leagues that led directly to the WPL, the English Women's Premier League.

In addition, amid the unpredictable chaos that is football, they had somehow managed to land a top-class coach: Johnny 'The Hardman' Dexter; one-time captain and hero of the local men's team, Melchester Rovers. One-time England international.

Rocky watched as her pass soared high, then Ffion rose, beating a defender who was trying to pull her shirt to stop her leaping. The ball ricocheted off Ffion's head, falling to Rocky's feet.

Perfect. As planned. Rocky felt a burst of adrenaline that she channelled into what she needed to do next. Onto it, with a sudden explosion of speed and power, Rocky was still shoulder-to-shoulder with a stocky Hebden midfielder whilst simultaneously tracking Ffion's run.

Three…

Two…

One…

Rocky side-footed the ball as Ffion broke away past the Hebden defence and, one-on-one with the keeper, slotted the ball home.

GOAL!

Perfectly slotted away by a footballer at the top of her game.

Hebden 0-4 Sowerby.

Normally Rocky would have gone to celebrate the goal with her captain. But she was on the ground, staring back at the sky. The midfielder she'd run parallel with had hit her hard, but not until she'd played the ball.

After punching the air and letting out a wild cheer, Rocky rolled over as the referee strode towards the offending Hebden player, who was being pushed by Charlotte Duncan and Nadiya Hussain, two of Rocky's more combative teammates.

Rocky could predict what would happen now too.

The ref would stop, thrust a yellow card at the Hebden player – then, after an exquisite pause, pull a red card out. The Hebden player would shout a rude word, then storm off, giving Rocky a dark look as she left the pitch.

Rocky sat up to watch.

Yellow card.

Red card.

Off.

Swear word.

Dark look.

In a way Rocky took the Hebden player's sending off as more meaningful than the 4-0 scoreline. Wasn't it good if the player who was been assigned to mark you got sent off? Rocky thought so. She was pleased to note that it was the third time it had happened this season.

Rocky's secret desire was to have two players sent off in one game because of her. Now *that* would be really satisfying.

Or would it?

Was it *kind* to want your opponents to be so bamboozled by your ballplay that they were ordered off before the end of the game? Rocky smiled. There was no room for worrying about kindness on the football pitch. Off it, maybe. But, on it, for Rocky Race, football was all about winning. Fairly. Or as close to fairly as you could get.

'On your feet, Race,' came the shout. 'Or are you mortally wounded? Or daydreaming?'

Rocky heard the booming voice of her coach, Johnny Dexter, chiding her.

He was right, of course. What *was* she doing? The game had fifteen minutes left and there she was – taking a rest, daydreaming, like he said – when she should be back in position, giving it anything and everything to not concede a goal.

Shortly after kick-off she realised that the game was changing: Hebden had started to get more of the ball and events were taking part increasingly in Sowerby's half.

Johnny Dexter's booming voice came at the team again.

'Keep the clean sheet!' he bellowed. 'Stop coasting. I want to see one hundred per cent commitment.'

Rocky glanced over at Coach. Johnny Dexter stood there, next to a woman in a tracksuit that Rocky had never seen before. Coach did not look happy. Rocky felt all her adrenaline and elation drain away. She shivered. Drew a deep, steadying breath. This game wasn't over. There was no way they were going to concede a goal and disappoint Coach.

Hebden were firing in high long balls, hoping for a slice of luck or a Sowerby mistake. Presumably they thought that if they did it five or six times they'd get a break, or at least a shot on goal.

Rocky was forced to play deeper. And deeper. No more feeding Ffion from central midfield, now she was a defender. And it frustrated her. Because Rocky believed that the best way of defending was attacking. If your opposition are defending, how can they attack you? It was simple. She'd heard Vic – Ffion's brother – say that once. And, although she would never admit it to anyone in the world, she looked up to Vic Guthrie.

He was tough.

He was uncompromising.

But he was the last person she wanted to be compared to at the moment. Maybe before. She would have liked to be compared to him before. But not now.

Now, another Hebden high ball causing a scramble in the penalty area. Rocky on the eighteen yard line, a Hebden striker arrowing in with no marker to tackle her and crucially Lily Halifax, the Sowerby keeper, off her line, stranded.

An open goal.

Only one way to stop it.

Block.

With another explosion of adrenaline, Rocky threw herself down, full-length, in front of the ball as the Hebden striker lined up her shot. And – in slower than slow motion – Rocky saw the underside of her boot coming at her head.

Then she heard a crack.

2

FOR WHATEVER REASON, Rocky didn't want to get up straight away.

She knew why she was on the floor, gazing at the darkening sky. The Hebden striker had been about to score. Lily Halifax was out of her goal mouth. And Johnny Dexter had been shouting 'Clean sheet... clean sheeeeeeeeet.'

So Rocky had had no choice. Even if she had to hurl herself in front of a set of striker's studs, she would do it. Which she did, the studs grazing the top of her head, sending her rolling onto the penalty spot.

19

It didn't hurt. Injuries never really hurt during a game because Rocky always felt she was flying. It made her wonder why professional footballers rolled around like they were in agony. Well, the men did.

But the way people were standing over her made Rocky want to remain lying there, looking up. She focussed in on a face she recognised. Ffion's. Then she identified the Hebden striker, who had nearly taken her head off, her face lined with worry.

Rocky smiled. Felt a bit dizzy. Then a weird memory popped into her head. The kind of memory that makes you feel you are back there. It was something that had happened a few days ago, but something that kept coming back, kept taking her by surprise.

Rocky is looking in through a window at three people she knows. And knows well.

One of them is shouting at a second. A third stands in between the other two. One is holding a TV remote in her hand. Then there is a flash as the first moves quickly, the second falls on the floor. A shout. A scream. More shouting. More screaming.

Then a crack as someone is punched. That's how Rocky remembers it.

She wouldn't forget. Not the punch. Not the scream. And not the feeling of horror and shock that someone she thought a lot of could do that to someone she loved. She shivered again at the memory.

'Can you hear me, Rocky?'

It was Ffion's voice, calling her back to the game, to the present.

' 'Course I can,' Rocky slurred. 'I'm not deaf.'

'You've got a cut on your head.'

Rocky sat up and touched her forehead.

It was wet. She looked at her fingers. They glistened red. She felt dizzy again and slightly nauseous.

But she didn't want to be dizzy, she didn't want to go off, so she stood up and wiped her forehead with the bottom of her football shirt to get rid of the blood, to make it look like she was okay.

They'd be worried about blood and

concussion. And that was the last thing she wanted. She hated being subbed off. Not playing the full ninety minutes was worse than losing for Rocky. Even though they were winning – and would win easily – she needed to be part of the full ninety.

'Is it a corner?' Rocky asked Ffion, backing away to take up position near the penalty spot, making it clear she wanted to play on.

Ffion was laughing now.

'What?' Rocky grunted.

'You're bleeding.'

'And?'

'And you might be concussed… so you can't play on.'

'No way,' Rocky complained. 'I'm fine, look.' She wiped her forearm on her head now. It was still dripping with blood. 'It's nearly stopped.'

'Hospital,' Ffion ordered.

'Hospital? I don't need...'

Rocky glanced over at her mum and dad, sitting by the car. Dad in a wheelchair. Mum in a deckchair, reading one of the books she was studying now she was taking night classes at college. Both of them were gesturing for Rocky to come off. She was surprised to see them there: she'd been so involved in the game that she had forgotten they were watching.

'You do, love,' the woman who had kicked her in the head countered. 'You'll need stitches on your forehead. You go now. I am so sorry. I feel bad enough as it is, so please go. There'll be a scar if you don't.'

Rocky felt herself being lifted to her feet.

'Oh no.' She pretended to be distressed. 'Won't I be beautiful anymore?'

Now she heard laughter from the players around her. Then applause as she trudged off.

'We could do with a player like you on our team,' the Hebden striker told her, still laughing, as they walked towards Johnny Dexter. Rocky made a mental note to ask him who the woman in the tracksuit was who was. Then mum was beside her and guiding her to the car.

AT A&E TWO hours later Rocky looked groggily at the red and yellow bunting around the reception area. She saw posters of Melchester Rovers too. One of Roy, signed with a Sharpie. And a full size copy of the League Cup, made from cardboard covered in silver foil, with red and yellow ribbons attached.

Johnny Dexter grinned. 'What a week,' he muttered to himself. 'I am so happy for the lads. For your Roy.'

Rocky smiled. She felt a little dizzy, but that was normal: she had a touch of concussion. She was trying to remember what she had wanted to ask Coach after she had come off. Something to do with a woman. But it had gone. As if the memory had been wiped out.

She felt a thrill of excitement seeing all the Melchester Rovers posters and hearing Coach talk about it. Seven days to go until the League Cup Final. League One Melchester Rovers versus Burndean of the Premier League. Even though her head hurt like hell, Rocky Race was buzzing.

Rocky stood in her bedroom, facing the mirror on the back of her closed door. Tucked behind the top corner of the mirror there was a ticket. It was white with the words Burndean versus Melchester Rovers. League Cup Final. 1st March 2020.

But – as excited as she was about going to watch her team play at Wembley for the first time – Rocky found herself staring at her reflection.

At her face. The one she didn't recognise anymore.

The pale skin. The dark expressionless

eyes peering back at her. A nose. A mouth. A chin. A school uniform: black skirt, black blazer, white shirt, blue and yellow tie. A uniform that she loathed. For a moment she studied her Doc Marten boots. Then she looked at the bandage on her head.

Her chest fluttering more and more, Rocky stepped closer to the mirror and ripped the bandage half off so she could see her wound: five stitches high on her forehead just below her hairline. She pressed the bandage back around the edges of the wound, then made to leave the room.

That was when the fluttering became breathlessness, then became like a punch in the chest. As she reeled backwards and sat on her bed, she tried to breathe in. But it was like her mouth and nose were closed. Nothing was going in. She grabbed her head and pulled her hair back to end the pain that was now jabbing in her chest like a hot knife in her heart. It had happened before: the shortness of breath. But not like this. Not like she thought she was going to black out, fall down, die.

Rocky took her time to count to ten, then up to twenty. She breathed in slowly to try to beat the pain.

And it worked.

Her head was not exploding now. Her eyes were not swimming. She was breathing.

What was this? Why did this keep happening? And why, this time, had it been so much worse?

Was this going to happen again?

She breathed in through her mouth, out through her nose. Nice and slow. She knew this was a way to calm yourself down. Shaking still, but faintly elated at being able to breathe, she wondered: did other people get this? It made no sense. There had to be a proper reason for her to feel like this, didn't there?

It wasn't the head wound: she wasn't bothered about that.

She had looked up her symptoms. Lots of her friends did it.

They fed their symptoms into the search engine on their computers and it spat out the worst case scenario possible. Rocky's beating heart, stabbing pains in the chest, breathlessness and her dry mouth were, apparently, signs of something in-between Post Traumatic Stress Disorder, heart disease and panic attacks. But Rocky was sensible enough to know that she did not have PTSD. And probably not heart disease.

So... panic attacks?

That's what she had.

Maybe.

What she was sure about was that it was getting harder and harder to walk out of her bedroom and do things she had never even thought about before. She wondered if today was the day she wouldn't be able to pull the door handle and walk out of the house.

It had started to happen a while ago. Just the fluttering at first. When her dad got ill. When Mel Park burned down. When she'd gone over the wall and stolen a file from Barry Cleaver's car and realised how insane that had been the next morning. She felt like she was a character in a book who has more and more difficult things to deal with. Until she breaks.

She felt like she was breaking now.

The last thing had really got to her: the day she'd gone to see Ffion at her house. Ffion had just been selected as Wales U18 captain and Rocky wanted to take her a card. Just to say well done. But, when she'd got to Ffion's and was walking up the path to deliver the card, she'd heard shouting coming from inside the semi-detached house. So loud she could hear it word for word through the closed window.

First Ffion's voice.

Then Vic's voice.

Then Roy, her brother's, voice.

Rocky had not known what to do. She wasn't used to rows at home. In their house – since their dad had been so ill, his speech silenced – there were no arguments. Not proper ones. Not since his brain tumour operation had left him barely able to say two words a week and half his body paralysed.

So, hearing shouting, Rocky froze and stared in through the front room window to see them standing in a triangle in front of the TV. Vic shouting at Ffion. Roy between them, looking uneasy.

What Rocky saw next seemed to happen in slow motion.

After a tirade of shouting, Vic pushed his sister. Not hard, but enough for her to drop the TV remote she was holding and enough, too, to anger Roy, who objected by putting his arm between the Guthrie siblings. Then Vic drew his arm back.

It was a brutal full-fisted punch.

Rocky couldn't see her brother through the window anymore. But she could hear shouting and screaming. And, before she could do anything more, the front door burst open and Vic Guthrie ran past Rocky, ignoring her, clearly not even seeing her, sobbing so hard she could still hear him as he ran down the street and into the distance.

It wasn't that Roy had been punched that upset Rocky. He was on his feet soon enough, getting lots of attention from Ffion.

The truly upsetting thing had been the look on Vic's face as he ran by. Here was someone she admired. Vic Guthrie was tough, like her. He was feisty, like her. He was strong and wilful and brave and funny. Like her.

She had thought they were alike.

Until this.

So why was he running down the street sobbing?

Why had he punched someone pretty harmless like Roy?

Why, in the weeks before, had he pushed a referee on the pitch and been banned for ten games? The kind of thing that happened in English football once a decade. But not to people like Vic.

It had opened up a Pandora's Box of question after question for Rocky.

People like Vic and Rocky didn't lose it. Did they?

People like Vic didn't stand inside their bedroom panicking that they couldn't even leave the house. Did they? Was he like that? Pretending to be wild and outrageous? What if Vic was scared of walking out of his bedroom? What if he really had to force himself to be Vic the tough-tackling, tough-talking midfielder? And what if sometimes he didn't manage it and that made him push referees and scream in his sister's face like a maniac and punch his teammates?

What if that sort of thing was going to happen to her?

ROCKY STARED HARD at her reflection, intending to make herself angry. She decided to think about school and how much she hated it. That could work.

She thought about how she felt she was on a conveyor belt of doing exam after exam after exam. SATs. GCSEs. A-levels. None of which she wanted to do. What she really wanted to do was something else, something that wasn't about reading books and then writing stuff down about the books.

The anger came easily. That surge of frustration. Then a spark.

Rocky grabbed her door, swung it open, thundered downstairs, snatched her coat from the hooks by the front door and slammed it behind her. She did all this so rapidly to make sure that no-one would see her, talk to her, ask her if she was alright and she'd have to say yes she was okay, when she *wasn't* okay. To avoid explaining how she felt. What was the point in talking about how you felt?

Rocky knew that some days could be better days without having to say goodbye to anyone at all. No chance for disagreement with her mum. No need for banter with her brother. Not even a hug with her dad – because it sometimes made her feel sad that he used to walk her to school and now he could not.

So, yes, sometimes, it was simpler to just walk out and grab something to eat at the shop or in school before the lessons kicked in. She could feel bad about it later.

Rocky climbed the long terraced street up the hill towards school and the Moor. She walked fast, putting pressure on her calves, then her thighs, using the ten-minute walk to build some strength in her legs. Every few houses she would see red and yellow flags and scarves. That – at least – had cheered her up. Six days to the cup final, she thought.

Imagine if they won. Imagine a bus top tour round the streets of Melchester. How amazing would that be?

And to see all these flags and this bunting. It was awesome. She had had no idea there were so many Rovers fans on her street. She smiled. This was good. Really good. See, the day was going okay.

At each side-street she passed, Rocky was joined by more children in black blazers and skirts or trousers that she had to overtake. She kept her head down. She didn't want to speak to anyone. She always did her best to walk alone and so fast that she overtook dozens of other children, especially the tiny year sevens who looked half the size of some of the year elevens and sixth formers.

No-one overtook Rocky Race between her house and school.

No-one ever did.

Just as she was approaching the school gates, she saw something out of the corner of her eye. Up against a wooden garden fence, hidden from the teachers under the school sign, there were four children. Most of them were year nines, she reckoned.

Three boys had another up against the fence. The other, a boy on his own, was pale and flinching as if he was about to be punched. He was year seven. It was obvious what was going on.

'Hey!' Rocky shouted.

One of the attackers had drawn his arm back to strike. As soon as he heard Rocky his arm fell to his side.

Rocky moved quickly. She recognised one face.

'You're Emma Granger's brother,' she shouted.

'So?' the boy said.

The boy glanced at his mates and smirked. They were all looking at her bandage.

'Do you know who I am?' Rocky smiled, peeling off her bandage, showing her wound.

'Er… you're… you're… Rocky Race.'

Rocky nodded. 'Very good. Now listen to me… I am filled from the crown to the toe top-full of direst cruelty and, if I see

you or hear of you having a go at a year seven again, I'll tell Emma and I'll tell your head of year and have you expelled. Do you understand?'

The three year nines paled, then ran.

Rocky was left standing with the trembling year seven.

'What's your name?' she asked him.

'Sam. Sam Lacey.'

'Well, Sam Lacey... if you or any of your mates have any trouble again, you come to me,' Rocky said. 'Okay?'

'Okay. I will,' Sam said. 'Thank you.'

IN REGISTRATION ROCKY sat next to Irfan Gatrad. He was the only one in her form group that she got on with. All her mates were in other forms. But she was lucky with Irfan. For a boy, he was tolerable. He was kind, too. So polite it was painful. As he sat down his eyes widened.

'Rocky!? What happened to you?' he said too loudly.

Rocky heard the scrape of chairs as others turned to see what Irfan was talking about.

'I got kicked in the head,' Rocky smiled.

Silence.

'Er... by who?' Irfan pressed.

'A defender.'

'Why did he do that?'

'He?' Rocky raised an eyebrow.

'I mean she,' Irfan blushed. 'I mean she... Sorry...'

'To be fair,' Rocky interrupted. 'It was my fault.'

'I thought your brother was the footballer,' a voice said from the pair of desks in front of them.

Rocky didn't reply, but she looked at Irfan

44

and rolled her eyes. She couldn't wait to get out of this place. In three months she would be taking her GCSEs, then she could leave.

She'd been at the school since she was 11, the same size as those little year sevens she'd powered past this morning on the hill. She'd always been known as Rocky Race, the feisty one you don't mess with. Or over the last year or so, the famous footballer Roy Race's sister. To some she was the girl whose dad was in a wheelchair and couldn't speak.

Likes football. Doesn't have a boyfriend. Good at sport and science. Terrible at art. The kind of girl who'll do A-levels, then maybe go to university and be something like a PE teacher. After her GCSEs.

Was that getting to her? Rocky wondered.

I thought your brother was the footballer.

How annoying was that?

If she was a boy she'd be able to leave

school and get a place at a football academy, an Under-18 contract, try her hardest to make a living playing the game she loved.

But Rocky Race was a girl.

Could that happen for a girl in a world that took much more notice of men playing football than it did of women?

Since her dad had been ill, Rocky had two ways she found that she could really connect with him, even though it was very difficult to have a conversation with words.

One was when she made fun of or argued with Roy and Dad laughed. For instance when she stole the food off his plate or squirted water at him from a bottle.

Two was watching films.

On Sunday afternoons, if there was no big game and Dad and Roy weren't playing FIFA, Rocky and her dad would watch films. War films. Over the months they'd watched most of the classics.

Saving Private Ryan.

The Dam Busters.

Battle of Britain.

They would both get onto the sofa and snuggle, shoulder to shoulder, and Rocky would feel good. Really good. Because it felt like things used to when she was a little girl

and her dad would hug her and they'd watch *Peppa Pig*, or, when Mum wasn't around, *The Simpsons.*

They been watching a film called *Carve Her Name with Pride* for an hour when Rocky turned to her dad. The film was about a woman called Violette Szabo, who fought the Nazis in World War Two.

'Why aren't there more films about women soldiers?' she asked.

Dad's face creased up and he looked – for a half-second – sad. Rocky forgot this sometimes. Stupidly. That he couldn't answer. That he'd want to answer. That he knew loads about war and used to love to talk about soldiers he admired. What dad wouldn't want to tell his daughter the exciting things she wanted to know? What dad wouldn't be deeply frustrated?

Rocky was desperate to make her dad

feel happy, to stop him being frustrated. She tried to imagine what he would be wanting to say, then had a go at saying it.

'Is it because women aren't soldiers? Maybe that's it?' Rocky speculated, trying to say the things she thought he would say back to her, ignoring the fact that Roy had just sidled into the room and slumped on the spare armchair.

'Are now,' Dad forced.

'Women are now? On the front line? Is that what you mean?'

Dad nodded.

'Yeah, but not many women make it,' Roy said idly from his armchair.

'What?' Rocky narrowed her eyes and studied her brother.

'Not many women make it,' Roy repeated. 'They need to pass tests to show they are as strong and fierce as men.'

'And…?'

'And women are weaker than men,' Roy informed his sister with a mischievous grin aimed at Dad.

Rocky heard Dad chuckle. He was clearly looking forward to a Rocky v Roy argument.

'So… I can't be in the army, but you can?' Rocky asked her brother in a pretend friendly tone that he would know was veiled with hostility.

Roy shrugged and looked at the screen. 'Chances are…' he muttered.

Rocky could see she had Roy rattled. He was being defensive now.

'Look at this film. Do you reckon you're more likely to be able to do that? Or me?'

'It's hypothetical,' Roy said.

'So… just answer me.'

'Neither of us could do that. Look at her. Jumping out of aeroplanes. Machine gunning

Germans with a shoulder wound. Facing a firing squad. It's terrifying. It's almost impossible,' Roy snapped, still staring at the screen.

'I could,' Rocky said. 'I would. I'd do it. And you wouldn't. You just said.'

Roy didn't reply.

'Roy?' Rocky pressed.

'I'm stronger than you,' he said. 'I'm male. Males are stronger.'

Rocky glanced at Dad. She could see he was still amused, enjoying the banter.

'You might be,' Rocky snapped. 'Physically. But there's more to strength than a few pounds of muscle. Mentally I could destroy you and all your teammates. My will power is phenomenal. I could jump out of a plane with a machine gun. You'd run for the hills.'

Silence.

'Well?' Rocky insisted.

Roy turned and gazed at his sister. 'Yeah. You're right. You would.'

Rocky studied her brother. He looked like the pale year seven she'd seen at the school gates. Suddenly, Rocky had another memory of seeing him being punched that night by Vic and she felt herself wobble deep down.

Was he thinking about that? Did he think he was weak? He had no idea she had seen him floored by Vic Guthrie. Had she gone too far? Yes, she had. She'd hurt his feelings. Properly. Arghhh. This was driving her mad: now she was feeling sorry for her brother, worrying about him. Why was she becoming so caring?

Rocky glanced at Dad and caught a worried look in his eye.

She knew what her dad was saying without having to think about it. Roy had a game in a couple of days. A midweek match. Rocky should lay off him.

'You're strong,' Rocky said, changing her tune. 'In lots of ways. Look what you've achieved. With everything that's gone on at Mel Park and here at home. You're amazing, Roy.'

Rocky saw Roy glance at her as if to mean *Why is she saying that? Why is she being caring?*

After an uneasy silence the three of them stared at the screen and, once the film had finished, no-one wanted to talk about it any more.

IT WAS THE last Melchester Rovers home game before the cup final and – as a result – the atmosphere was jumping.

In town.

Outside the stadium.

In Mel Park itself.

This football club – once one of the greatest in Europe – had suffered years of decline. Then it had been involved in events that could have seen the club wiped off the face of the earth. In fact, that could still happen. But not if Rovers won the cup.

No.

At the beginning of the season, Melchester Rovers had been docked thirty points. This was because their owner – Barry Cleaver – had lied and cheated, then tried to burn Mel Park down. It had seemed to Melchester Rovers fans that their club was in its death throes.

But they'd been lucky.

After a police investigation, Barry Cleaver had been charged by the police with arson, corruption and a dozen other crimes. And there had been more good news. Without a football ground to play in, their neighbours, Tynecaster United, had offered their stadium for Melchester to use. For free.

A mixed blessing to be in the debt of your greatest rival, but better than going out of existence. And one amazing thing at the Tynecaster Stadium was the area set aside for wheelchair users and their families. It was under cover with outdoor heaters. There was a space for the wheelchair user and three family members to sit with them. Tynecaster United were the devil's team, but this was one thing Rocky had to give them credit for.

And – since Melchester Rovers had been given their thirty points back – they'd been flying. Instead of being bottom of the table, they were top half and pushing towards the playoffs. Their latest game was at home to Queen's Park. Rocky Race sat next to her dad and mum in the disabled supporters' enclosure. Rovers were 2-0 up. She loved it when it was like this at the football.

Winning. On the up. A sniff of success. Nothing negative to make her worry they might lose or get relegated or go out of business. Things were good. That was what she loved about watching the football, like playing it. It became everything. There was nothing else. Just the intake of breath before a goal, then leaping about wildly celebrating.

'We could be in the Championship next season,' she enthused to her dad, who winked at her with his good eye.

'We'll be back in the Prem soon,' Rocky went on, filling in the gaps. 'Two seasons. Three at the most…'

'And at Mel Park, too,' Mum added.

Rocky was about to rant about how Melchester Rovers now had to play at the ground of their great rivals, Tynecaster United. But her reply was drowned out by a noise from the crowd, Rocky turning to see Asif Mirza bursting down the left, his red and yellow strip ripping up the lush green grass.

'Go on, Race,' a drunken voice from the seats directly behind them shouted. 'In the box. Attack.'

Rocky studied the shape of the game as Roy tracked parallel with Mirza, watching the Queen's Park defensive line carefully. Roy always did this, running the line until the pass came in, then using his exceptional pace to get on the end of a pass or cross ahead of a defender.

'Get your hat-trick, mate,' another voice added.

The noise levels rose even more in the Tayir Stadium as Mirza unexpectedly cut the ball back to Patrick Nolan, forcing the Queen's Park defence to hesitate, confused, no longer playing as a unit. Roy hesitated too, but only long enough to keep him onside; then he followed in Nolan's chip as it looped perfectly into his path. Two defenders cut out of the game by a single pass and Roy one-on-one with the keeper, his body leaning right, the ball rolling left, touching off the post. And in. She had no idea how he'd scored it, but Rocky punched the air all the same. Mum too. Then they both hugged Dad.

Rocky heard herself above the noise of the crowd, her own voice roaring, echoing back at her from thousands of other Melchester Rovers fans.

3-0.

Game over. Elation. Glory. Perfection. Joy.

Maximum points.

Climbing two places up the league.

After celebrating his goal, Roy did what he always did now when he scored. He ran over to his dad and pointed at him, for a second, Dad raising his right arm in a salute.

Rocky heard voices behind them muttering about whether the girl with dark hair and the guy in the wheelchair were Roy's family.

But she ignored them and focussed on being in the moment.

A beery voice behind Rocky burst the bubble.

'You're Roy Race's sister, aren't you?'

Rocky turned round. Mum too.

'That's right,' Mum said. 'I'm his mum. How are you?'

Rocky knew what Mum was doing: taking over the conversation, moving it away from the whole *You're Roy's sister* thing. At least one person got her. Sometimes.

'A first half hat-trick,' the man purred, still insisting on talking to Rocky. 'You must love your big brother.' Then he put his hand on her shoulder.

Rocky snapped, shrugging him off. 'No. He's a clown,' she said, surprised by her rage towards the man surging up in her. 'In fact, he's the worst. He *sucks*.'

Rocky's head hurt. Her whole body was flushed with anger. She felt the urge to stand up and punch the man, swing her arm like Vic had swung his. But she just glared at him, trembling.

The man faked a smile and eased back into his seat, silent, cowed.

Rocky sat down and breathed deeply. In,

then out. In, then out. Her mind was working out what could have happened next. She was troubled. What if she *had* turned round and punched the man? Could she really do it? She wanted to. She really wanted to. What he'd said. Him touching her like that. Was that enough to justify punching him? And what did that mean, that she had urges like that?

That she had changed? That she was like Vic?

Once again, all her good feelings drained away. She felt ice cold and her hands were trembling. She hated this. This weirdness.

Rocky stood up quickly. 'I'm going home,' she told her mum.

'What? Why?' Mum stood up too. 'It's not even half-time.'

'To revise,' she said, though it wasn't true.

'We'll all come,' Mum said, Dad nodding

agreement. 'I need to revise too. I've got these entry exams coming up...'

'No,' argued Rocky. 'I'll get the bus. It's ten minutes. You can revise tomorrow and Roy will be disappointed if you go. And we've won. It's 3-0. You could be about to see a six or a seven-nil. And I need to do some... I don't know... some Chemistry.'

ROCKY FOUND HERSELF facing the mirror on
the back of her bedroom door again.

Thursday morning and she was the only
one up after the match the night before. She
looked hard at her face. It was pale. Her
nose looked a funny shape. And then there
was her shoulders. Had they always been
so droopy? Why did this happen every day
now? She barely recognised herself, hated
what she looked like, when she'd never ever
been bothered about what she looked like
before.

Or was it she didn't recognise how she

behaved – wanting to hit a man – being angry all the time? Wasn't that even more worrying than appearances?

And here it was again: that surge of panic, heart hammering, breath short, the overwhelming urge to fall back on her bed, switch the light off and pretend she wasn't there.

Not today. She didn't want it today. She put her hands on her knees and breathed in and out, slower and slower, until she felt calm again.

Did everyone have to fight like this? she wondered. Did everyone start the day forcing themselves to open a door?

Rocky shrugged. She had no idea, but she knew she had to go to school. The morning would be as dull as usual, but, at least, this afternoon would be better. The head of English – Miss Housego – was taking them to see a film called *Little Women*. That might be fun.

And, anyway, if she didn't go to school it would show on her record she'd missed another day. When she went for that interview at the A-level college they'd want to know why she'd missed so many days. Then they might not let her do A-levels. Then she'd be doomed.

'Like I want to do A-levels anyway,' she said to her reflection.

But her reflection didn't reply: it just stared, dull-eyed, back at her.

Rocky snatched at the door handle, her fingers trembling, ready to storm down the stairs.

'Bye Mum! Bye Dad!' she shouted into their bedroom. Then, walking past Roy's room, she stopped, a grin creeping across her face. Roy was having a lie-in. A day off after a match. Last night he had scored four goals to keep Rovers in the hunt for the playoffs. Who in Melchester deserved a lie-in more than Roy Race?

She did.

Rocky smashed her brother's door open and saw him sit up in fear. She already felt better. It was mean and it was cruel, but

harassing her older brother was one of the bright sparks in her life.

'Whaaaaat?' he moaned.

'Kick-off's in ten minutes!' Rocky shrieked. 'You're late! For the cup final! You've blown it!'

'No… I…' Roy was fighting off his duvet to get up.

'Now you're on the pitch and you're taking a penalty… and you've missed! You've missed, Roy!'

Roy was on his feet.

'Noooo… Whaaaat…. I… I don't understand.'

'And now there's a rabbit in the kitchen,' Rocky was laughing. 'And it wants answers!'

Roy Race was standing in his boxers now, his head in his hands, his eyes wild and mouth open.

'Morning, Roy,' Rocky grinned and

left him to it, laughing hard, feeling okay, until she was on the other side of the front door and the smile slid from her face and she wondered why she did things like that. Why? Why had she always had a go at her brother? Why did he always take it and laugh along? And – most worrying of all – why did it make her feel better? For a while, at least.

A MORNING AT school. An afternoon at the cinema.

And, after the film, Rocky walked directly home on her own through town. She passed three Costa Coffees, two MacDonald's and one Army Recruitment Office. She was walking fast and thinking hard.

Little Women had been amazing. Or – more so – the main character had been amazing. She was called Jo March. It was set in the olden days in America, where a girl reached fifteen and had to start to think about marriage and a rubbish job like being a governess or a teacher.

But Jo March didn't go along with what she was supposed to do.

She had a dream: she wanted to be a writer.

Rocky didn't want to be a writer. She couldn't think of a job that would be more boring than that. She'd rather be a teacher! Imagine sitting at a desk or a table all day writing hundreds, maybe thousands, of words. The idea made her want to cry. But that wasn't it. This Jo March... she had done the opposite of what she was *supposed* to do.

That was what had excited Rocky. That was why she was walking fast and powerfully up the Terrible 200 as if they weren't even there.

Now all she had to do was work out what the opposite of doing two years of A-levels then going to university, then the rest, was supposed to be…

THAT EVENING, BEFORE kick off in Sowerby FC's next match, Johnny Dexter took Rocky aside and went down on one knee in front of her. Time for one of his one-to-one pep talks. Time for some motivational mumbo-jumbo, she knew. And she liked that sort of thing. But, still, she couldn't stop herself having a gentle go at Coach as he was still down on one knee.

'I won't marry you, if that's what you're thinking,' Rocky snapped. 'You're not really my type.'

When Johnny Dexter had stopped

laughing, he put his hand on Rocky's shoulder, looking into her eyes.

'You're too good for me, Rocky Race,' he said. 'But, tell me, how are things at home?' he asked.

'Better than they were,' Rocky replied, not wanting to talk about it. 'Dad's improving. Mum's at college and a bit intense about it, you know?'

'Good. Good,' her Coach went on. 'I know. I know. And how about at school?'

'I hate it,' Rocky said, surprising herself. 'I really hate it.'

Coach nodded, looked at the ground, then back at Rocky.

'Why are you asking me all this?' Rocky asked.

'It's my job.'

'Is it?'

'And I care about your family. You and Roy, your mum with her going back to college and your dad recovering from his illness. You need the likes of me watching out for you. There were times when I was a bit lost off the pitch,' he went on. 'And I found that I could leave it behind once I was on the pitch – that it made me feel better all round.'

'So?'

'So, that last game,' Coach said gently. 'You looked a bit lost every now and then, like you were daydreaming.'

'Did I?' Rocky asked.

She had no idea she had come across like that. She had maybe been a bit distracted, but that was all. Was the Vic thing really getting to her that much that Coach would think that she was daydreaming? The last thing she wanted was for life to interfere with football. She had thought that she was free of everything when she was playing. But maybe not. Maybe Coach had spotted something.

'I'm not lost,' Rocky said.

'No. I didn't mean...'

Rocky interrupted. 'So don't worry about it,' she said.

'I do, Rocky. I'm your coach.'

'Don't.'

'Just let me say, Rocky, that the pitch is a different space. If you can find something out there, away from school and home, it'll help you at school and home. If you find a space to be you, you can find a way of coping with the world and all the other people by having that special place. Like how I used to feel at Melchester Rovers. Understood?'

'Yeah, Coach,' Rocky said quickly, starting to feel anxious, wanting to stop this conversation. 'Can I warm up now?'

Johnny Dexter nodded. 'Go on. Shove off.'

THE MATCH BEGAN frenetically. The opponents – Todmorden – were pressing for every ball, giving Rocky and her teammates little time to think.

Rocky played hard, short passes, no-

nonsense tackles. Soon she had the midfield sewn up and Todmorden were backing off. And tiring. Even in the first half.

This was how you had to manage a tight game like this.

Keep it simple.

Make clear choices.

Focus on the basics.

Then wait for the game to open up.

She was still learning about team football. And fast. There clearly was something about playing full games week in week out that made you understand the game so much more than just watching it or playing during a school lunch break.

Because of the nature of the game, the first quarter passed rapidly. It was only once the game had calmed down that Rocky stopped to consider that Coach was right.

On the pitch things *were* different. On the

pitch they *were* glorious. She was in control. She knew her job. She didn't have time to worry if her face was pale or that she didn't like school or what she was going to do her A-levels in or if her dad was ill or how she felt being Roy's sister.

All she had to do was break up the Todmorden attacks before they started. Keep the ball moving. Make it impossible for Todmorden to settle.

But now she had more space, Rocky was able to be a little more creative too. Ffion – up front – had been starved of the ball. Rocky had heard her calling for it time after time. She wasn't even sure her captain had had a touch yet. This was ultra-frustrating for Rocky: she knew that they depended on each other on the pitch, that their games and goals depended on each.

Thirty minutes in, Rocky answered her

captain's call. Bursting through two tackles goal-side of the centre circle, Rocky played a short pass to her winger Nadiya Hussain, ran into space taking it back, then, seeing Ffion glide ahead, Rocky dinked a ball in front of her, leaving the defence tied up in knots.

The ball bounced once, twice, then Ffion hit it hard on the half volley, into the top corner of the goal.

1-0.

A cheer exploded from the dozens of fans watching. That was better. This was football. Football overriding everything.

Before half time Ffion and Rocky teamed up to score again. This time on the break. Helena Pielichaty hit a low fast ball from the Sowerby penalty area to Rocky, who, back to the ball, turned and powered forward, taking Todmorden by surprise.

We're so much fitter than them, Rocky thought as she cut through three, then four, opponents to see Ffion sprinting in from the left. Rocky moved right, drew the last defender and keeper with her, then poked a ball sideward.

All Ffion had to do was side tap it into an open goal.

2-0.

The Rocky and Ffion show was on the road.

Rocky heard more shouts from the touchline. She looked up to see Mum, Dad, her brother. All looking suitably happy.

Rocky beamed. *This* was it. *This* was what she wanted.

Victory. Happy faces. Nothing to worry about. She wished she could live her life on the football pitch. Then she'd stop panicking.

If only there was something she could do after her GCSEs that made her feel like this all the time. If only Ffion wasn't about to say what she was about to say.

'ROCKY?'

It was long after the game had ended and everyone was done and dusted in the changing room, well after most of the girls had headed home. In fact, Rocky thought she was the last. She was dragging her heels.

Hearing her name, though, Rocky turned.

It was Ffion. She was waiting under a floodlight, her long plaited red hair glowing in the artificial light. A fine rain was falling now, like invisible curtains being drawn across the night.

'I thought you'd gone off with Roy,' Rocky said.

'No.' Ffion shook her head. 'I need to talk to you.'

'Why?'

Ffion didn't reply. And Rocky said nothing more. Because she knew. Ffion had something to tell her. Something not good. It was obvious from Ffion's expression.

Sowerby had just won 4-0. Ffion normally looked pink-faced and elated after a win like that. Not hesitant, like now.

'I won't mess about,' Ffion said.

Rocky felt a flutter in her chest. *What was this? What was Ffion about to say that was so important?*

The answer came quickly.

'I've been offered a scholarship at Steinbeck University in America. They've got a professional team. I'll have a chance at making it as a pro. They'll put me through college. A proper education. And pay me, too. It's madness.'

Rocky said nothing.

'If I go...' Ffion said.

At first Rocky felt crestfallen. Ffion couldn't go. She wanted to say. *No. Don't go. You're the most important person in my life. Without you. Without Sowerby,*

85

I've nothing. Without you all I have got is problems.

But Rocky didn't say that. She merely mumbled: 'Right then. Well done.'

In fact, she felt a tiny bit of comfort that Ffion was telling her first. That was nice. That meant Rocky mattered to her.

Ffion was smiling now, encouraged. She carried on: 'And... I wanted to ask you if... when I should talk to Roy about it? I mean... before the cup final? Or after?'

'Oh...'

'What do you think?' Ffion asked, not sensing Rocky's sudden crushing disappointment that she was telling Rocky because she wanted to know when she should talk to Roy.

'I mean...' Ffion went on. 'I've not made my mind up if I should go and I need to talk to Roy to see what he thinks and if he can cope and I don't know if it'll be best just to leave it until Monday. You know, after the cup final.'

A car flashing its lights caught Rocky's eye. Then she saw Roy waving standing next to Mum's car. He was grinning.

'Rocky? You coming?' he shouted. 'Mum wants to get off.'

Rocky turned to study Ffion.

'I woke Roy up this morning,' she confessed. 'Way too early. I shouted loads of stuff at him to freak him out and he jumped out of his skin. I'm mean to him. But, look, he's not angry with me at all.'

'He told me,' Ffion smiled. 'He thought it was funny. You were going on about a rabbit in the kitchen.'

Rocky was gloomy now. Losing Ffion. Roy finding out the love of his life was leaving. Because she *would* go. Roy wouldn't stop her. He'd be all selfless and supportive and proud. And Ffion would be insane to give up this chance of a footballing lifetime. Rocky kind of felt sorry for her brother.

'He lets me get away with murder,' she said.

' 'Cos he loves you, Rock.'

Rocky shrugged. 'Whatever,' she muttered. She didn't like it when people talked about love.

'So?' Ffion pressed.

'So what?'

'So what do I do? Talk to him now? Or after?'

'After,' Rocky told her. 'We're only going to win the cup if he's in the zone.'

'Right.'

'See you,' Rocky said, then she jogged towards her mum's car. She felt sorry for Roy, yes. But she felt sorrier for herself now and needed to get away from Ffion. This was another thing she didn't have control over. And Rocky understood: she had to start to take control of things in her life before they took control away from her. But what? And how?

The rain on her face helped her keep her feelings to herself.

Mum and Dad were in the kitchen when Rocky came down for breakfast the next morning. Rocky grabbed a bowl of cereal and ate it rapidly, not wanting to talk. She sensed both her parents watching her.

She used to think her mum and dad could read her mind, and if she had a secret or a worry, they would just know. Like today. But now she knew that adults were just as clueless as children. There was no special way they could tell Rocky had two secrets bouncing around in her head.

She had learned this.

Like she had learned a lot recently.

'I need a screwdriver,' Rocky said, after drinking juice from the carton.

It was time to take control of one of the things that was making her feel like she was losing control.

'I've asked you not to do that,' Mum chided Rocky.

'Do what?'

'Drink juice from the carton.'

'Sorry. I won't do it again,' Rocky said, smirking at Dad.

Dad laughed.

'Middle drawer,' Mum sighed, pointing.

'Thanks.'

Rocky grabbed the screwdriver and ran up the stairs. Back in her room, after putting her cup final ticket on her bedside table – under the candle she'd been given for Christmas but wasn't allowed to light in her room –

she breathed in, gritted her teeth and, using the screwdriver, quickly detached the mirror from the back of her bedroom door.

This removing of the mirror was a big deal for Rocky. There'd been a change. She had taken control back of her life. Now the mirror was not going to be there on the door. The door was just a door. Something she could open without feeling bad.

But there was more. More control to be taken.

Last night. She'd known it last night too. She had gone to bed fuming, betrayed and lost. Ffion was leaving. Everything was terrible. She had lain in her bed scowling into the darkness of her room, thinking, Who the hell was Ffion to just go off and do something amazing for herself like that? What about everyone else? What about Rocky and Roy and Vic?

This went on until 3 a.m. And then it struck her.

Ffion was doing what she wanted.

Ffion was not doing what other people wanted.

Ffion had found something so good, no-one was going to be able to, or really want to, stop her doing it. Like that what's-her-name in *Little Women*. Jo so-and-so. She'd had a dream. She'd had an opportunity. And she'd taken it.

Rocky flicked her light switch on and grabbed her laptop. She keyed in

ALTERNATIVES TO A LEVELS.

That was what she needed. An alternative. Something that wasn't the boring future that was laid out for her.

This was another thing she was trying to take control of so that she didn't feel like it was controlling her.

She had read through a list of acronyms like BTEC, NVQ and a few others. They all sounded the same as A-levels to her, courses where she'd have to go to college for two years and learn things to do in exams that she'd never have anything to do with again.

A-levels with different names was all they were.

Why did children have to carry on in school or college until they were 18? Why was it illegal to just go and work somewhere?

Rocky was beginning to rage again. But, then, just as she was about to give up, an advert pinged up in the right hand column of the webpage. One of those adverts that the internet thinks you'll be interested in and you never are.

Until today.

Until she read the words:

THE ARMY FOUNDATION COLLEGE

What? Rocky read on.

At the Army Foundation College (AFC), Harrogate, we get 16 and 17 year olds ready for a career in the British Army. We can help you get the military skills, fitness and education that you need for a great start in whichever part of the Army suits you – while you earn a good wage and make friends for life.

Rocky grabbed the laptop and read the whole webpage. When she'd finished, she knew.

Education. She needed that.

Fitness. She had that already and wanted more.

Military skills. Why not? She loved the films she watched with her dad and wanted to be like Violette Szabo. Why not do it? Do it for real? Herself.

A good wage. Yes please.

Friends for life. Why not?

Rocky Race saw a new and exciting future

shimmering in front of her eyes. She would join the Army. As long as they let her play for Sowerby, then England. As long as she was allowed to be a footballer. Then everything would be perfect.

She had barely slept a wink all night.

Now she had her screwdriver and had removed the mirror from the back of her door, Rocky waited in her room for Roy to leave to travel to London to spend the night at a hotel near Wembley. She kind of wanted to say good luck, but she didn't want to face him knowing a secret that could devastate him and put him off his game.

Mum drove Roy to Mel Park. Then, before going to sit with her dad in the front room, Rocky nipped into Roy's room and carefully screwed the mirror onto the back of the door.

With a bit of luck he'd be able to look at his Cup Winner's Medal in the mirror on Sunday. He'd be thrilled, wouldn't he?

THE FOLLOWING DAY, Rocky, Mum, Dad and Johnny Dexter walked up Wembley Way side by side. But it didn't feel like walking at all. To Rocky it felt like she was on a wave that was carrying the four of them, and the other twenty thousand Melchester Rovers fans, up the famous walkway towards one of the best days of her life.

The League Cup Final, 2020.

Rocky was overwhelmed by red and yellow scarves and banners all around her. This was big. This was huge. After years of terrible football fortune, Melchester Rovers

were back in the big time. And – more so
– this was a game that, if they won (and
she knew they would), the club would win
prize money. That would mean they would
be saved because the new owners, whoever
they were, would not have to sell Mel Park
to build a supermarket or a housing estate,
because they would have the money to invest
in the club.

Simple.

They would win. They would survive. They would become a great club again.

Rocky caught her dad's eye as Johnny Dexter pushed his wheelchair at her side. This was massive for him too. Dad had been so ill and he seemed to be getting a bit better. Now he was able to go to all the Rovers games he wanted, having missed dozens. He must be loving this!

And now both Mum *and* Dad would see their child play at Wembley. How many parents got to do that? *How many get to see two of their children do it?* Rocky asked herself. That was what was next. She'd do it too. But not yet. That was for tomorrow. Today was about today. Today was about Roy.

'We're here,' she said to Dad. 'We're here.'

Dad smiled his half-smile, his eyes alive. 'Wembley,' he stuttered.

Rocky beamed. She caught mum's eye.

They both laughed. A word from Dad was good. But a two-syllable word! It was the first time he had done that since he'd been ill. It was a sign. Her dad was going to get better. Rovers were going to win the cup. Things were going to be okay.

Rocky was overwhelmed by a rush of euphoria. It was time for a song. And, if no-one else was going to do it, she would. She started singing:

'Wembley! Wembley! We're the famous Melchester and we're off to Wembley!'

Instantly, the chant spread like wildfire. Now thousands of Rovers fans were singing: 'WEMBERLEEE, WEMBERLEE, WE'RE THE FAMOUS MELCHESTER AND WE'RE OFF TO WEMBERLEE.'

This little bit of north west London was rocking. Dad was laughing now. Johnny Dexter too. And Mum.

'You started that, Dad,' Rocky said, leaning into her dad as they moved towards the national stadium. It was hard for her to hold back the tears. Watching Rovers in a cup final. With her mum and with Dad. This was a dream come true. Everything was coming together. She wondered if this was the happiest day of her life: it certainly would be, once they had lifted the cup.

Because the final was so important, she'd put the whole Army thing to one side for the day. She planned to ask Roy to talk to Mum about it. He might actually be able to help her persuade Mum. He could be useful. Sometimes.

INSIDE WEMBLEY, ROCKY felt almost too excited to be able to bear it. Here she was – in the section of the stadium put specially aside for families with a wheelchair user, right by the goal line – and her brother, their son, was in the March sunshine, stroking the ball to and fro with his attacking partner, Paco Diaz.

At one point, as the players warmed up in the spring sunshine, Roy came over to give them all a hug. Even Rocky. And, as he jogged back onto the pitch to warm up and, after the Melchester Rovers' coach, Kevin Mouse, had been over to greet them, she understood that this was probably one of the best days of her mum and dad's lives. Because, whatever happened to her dad, they would all have had this amazing day.

Their son, her brother, playing in a cup final at Wembley. In a game that, if they won, would secure the future of Melchester Rovers after two decades of nightmare scenes.

For their family, for their club, for their city, this was destiny.

They *would* win.

Rocky knew it. Because she knew she could see the future. This was her new ability.

The stage was set for red and yellow glory and Rocky Race allowed herself a smile.

BUT FOOTBALL IS not always that simple. It's unpredictable. It can even be unpleasant.

Everything happening on the Wembley turf was against the spirit of the game. Against the spirit of what Melchester Rovers prided themselves on. But – with a squad of high quality footballers – their opponents, Premier League Burndean, were absolutely brilliant at it.

Defensive overload. Cynical fouls. Fake injuries. Timewasting. Referee baiting. You name it. It seemed inspired by the worst World Cup group games you have ever watched or the most nervy anxious relegation six-pointers.

This was anti-football.

Rocky started the game shouting, complaining. But soon – like the Melchester team – she was lulled into a lethargy that had no place in a cup final.

The first half passed and, by its end, the euphoria of the walk up Wembley Way was wasted.

So, an hour later, with the second half kicking off, the score remained nil-nil. Melchester Rovers – who had promised to play their fluent carefree game in the press conferences before the game – had barely been able to get a shot on goal.

Burndean were playing deep, letting Rovers have the ball, but stifling them in their own half.

'Premier League?' Rocky raged. 'You're

having a laugh! Maybe mid-table, but we're League One. And they're... they're scared of us.'

Mum nodded. 'They're playing for penalties,' she said.

Rocky and Mum looked at Johnny for his view.

The big man shrugged. 'Just what you said,' he agreed. 'Your analysis is spot on. And the worse thing is, it's working.'

Rocky watched as Paco Diaz was blocked and tackled hard on the left wing for the twentieth time. And as Gordon Stewart's long clearances were dealt with by the two giant Burndean centre backs. All Melchester's usual ways of starting an attack were being stifled.

Roy had barely had a touch. And, when he moved back to try and get possession of the ball, he was shepherded away.

'He's not used to this level of defending,' Dexter muttered. 'It comes with experience. He's in above his head.'

Rocky saw Dad nod.

'But it'll come,' Dexter said. 'You only learn by facing adversity.'

A few minutes later, like most of the Rovers' players, the Burndean defenders were tiring. Rocky could see that.

'Roy's getting more of the ball,' she heard herself say as the volume of the Melchester fans increased. And it was true. The game, at last, was opening up. Burndean were being less guarded, creating space for Melchester to play their freewheeling game. But it also meant that Burndean were pushing forward and it was clear they had class, Premier League class that could help them cut Rovers to ribbons.

Rocky sat on the edge of her seat, obsessing

over the bounce of every ball, the movement of every player off it. Until it happened. The moment in the game that Melchester Rovers fans would be talking about for days, for weeks, for months.

Roy had been downfield to retrieve the ball, run with it. He'd played a one-two with Paco and found himself channelled towards the corner flag.

Rocky watched him spin, take the ball with him and dribble his way into the penalty area. It was too tight an angle to shoot, but he was in the danger zone at least. Roy surged again, trying to break away from the two defenders who had him shackled to the line.

Then the tackle came in. A defender caught the side of Roy's boot. Rocky watched as her brother stumbled, trying to keep his balance as the cry went up.

'PENALTY!' Rocky screamed, joining the choir of thousands.

She noticed too that the referee was moving his whistle towards his lips. This was it. This was the moment. When all Melchester Rovers' problems would be solved, when the world would be a better place for Rovers and for Rocky and her whole family. She felt like she was about to burst with excitement.

THE WHOLE STADIUM held its breath as Roy Race stumbled, regained his balance, and doggedly chased the ball towards the touch line until, agonisingly, it rolled out of play.

Now all eyes were on the ref. The penalty. Would he give it? He had to give it? Surely.

But the referee was jogging backwards to the half way line, pointing the way he had come. Indicating a goal kick. His whistle was in his hand, swinging at his side as he ran.

Now there was shouting.

But not in harmony. Hundreds of voices

were shouting at Roy, questioning Roy, blaming at Roy.

A cacophony of complaint.

Why had he not gone down? The referee was set to give a penalty. He had his whistle to his lips. Almost. All Roy needed to have done was follow his stumble through and fall. There had been a minute to go. The competition organisers would have been tying red and yellow ribbons to the trophy.

These were the things the Mel Park faithful were shouting out.

The things Rocky's parents were having to listen to.

These were the things going round Rocky's mind, too, as she watched Kevin Mouse, the Melchester Rovers' coach, staring hard at the players.

What was he thinking?

Was he thinking the same as the fans?

Why? Why didn't you just go down, Roy? You were fouled!

The inside of Rocky's head felt hot. Her eyes sore. She wanted to lash out. Scream. Shout. Hit. Hate. Rage. Something to release the pressure she felt building inside herself. Images of Roy and Ffion and Vic hammered around her head, too. This rage. Why couldn't it leave her alone?

Rocky looked at Mum and Dad in desperation. At Johnny Dexter too. None of them would catch her eye.

'We would have won the cup,' Rocky said to no-one.

And no-one answered.

'We wouldn't have gone out of business,' Rocky added. 'The prize money alone would have saved us…'

Then Rocky felt an arm around her. Mum's. But Rocky was too cross to want to be comforted, so she shrugged off the hug and watched hard as Lofty Peak challenged for the goal kick, only to see his header run on too far ahead of Roy.

Then Patrick Nolan being tackled as he tried to put another Melchester attack together.

The straw that broke the camel's back for Rocky was Nolan's next move.

Their Premier League opponents were taking the ball to the corner and shielding it from the Melchester players, even though the score was 0-0. Rocky was just thinking that Vic would have winkled that ball out: he would have found a way. But, here they were, unable to even get the ball. She realised how much the team missed their captain.

Then Nolan struck. A terrible tackle from a player who never normally tackled, to take the legs of the Premier League striker. Both legs. Hard. And now the Burndean player was writhing on the ground, like he'd been gunned down.

The ref sprinted over to them, holding something in the air.

A card.

Red.

Patrick Nolan was being sent off for the first time in his career.

The Rovers' fans were silent now. They had run out of rage. Rocky, though, still felt fury. And injustice. Now there was *no* way they could win. Ten League One players against eleven super-fit Premier League footballers.

It was over.

The only chant she heard was from the Burndean fans.

'One Roy Race!' they mocked. 'There's only one Roy Race!'

And, as she heard it, Rocky couldn't contain her anger towards her idiot brother.

This. Was. His. Fault.

She kicked out at the seat in front, her mum eyeing her with a silent warning.

Rocky had to get away from here. She felt a stab to her chest. Then another. Not this. Not again.

'I have to go to the loo,' she gasped, turning to walk up the steps to the entrance, just as the final whistle went, signalling extra time.

Fifteen minutes each way. Thirty minutes of agony. She knew it. Because Rocky Race could read the game so much better now.

She had seen that the Melchester players were tiring against the Premier League side. Seen how they were cramping. Premier League sides had all that science and knowledge to keep their players fitter than the Rovers boys could ever be. And against ten men? It was over.

They would not win the cup.

She listened to the Melchester fans, who were chuntering about how, if Race had gone down, they'd be celebrating winning the cup right now.

Rocky wasn't sure she would ever be able to forgive her brother.

ROCKY DIDN'T HESITATE when she left her bedroom the morning after the cup final.

Monday.

Who liked Mondays?

No-one. Usually. But Rocky had had an epiphany.

There was no mirror on the back of her door now, so she just opened her bedroom door, walked down the stairs, said goodbye to her mum and dad, then was off to school.

Things had changed. Since she had moved the mirror. Since she had decided to join the Army. Even though she had had the worst day yesterday, she still felt like she was in control.

She was astonished.

Roy was home really late the night before. The Melchester Rovers' bus had been caught on the motorway north in traffic. He got home after she'd gone to bed. That suited Rocky. She could hear the words she'd said to her dad at the match.

We would have won the cup.

We wouldn't have gone out of business.

Extra time had been a catastrophe. They had gone 1-0 down in five minutes. Then conceded two more as they chased the game, leaving great gaps at the back for the Premier League substitutes, all internationals, to exploit.

It was embarrassing. A 3-0 defeat?

When they should have, could have, *would have* won.

OUTSIDE, IT FELT like spring. It was March now. The long dark cold winter walks to school were forgotten. Every other garden on Rocky's way to school was packed with daffodils thrusting up towards the sun. And it was lighter and brighter and warmer now.

Spring.

She loved spring.

Even though Melchester had lost a cup final, Rocky Race felt good.

And her attitude was different now. She had done it. She had applied to be in the Army. Online. Last night.

That was why she felt better. Desperate remedies for desperate measures.

Everything would be different now. She

was going to work. Work hard. She would try so hard that she would pass English and Maths. She needed them. And she'd work hard at the sciences, in case, when she was in the Army, she would get opportunities to be an engineer or something like that. Why not? She could be anything! And, the better she did at school, the better chance she would have in the Army.

She would train harder at football too – with or without Ffion. Now she knew that there was a Women's Army Football Team who played in various tournaments. They even played against other countries. Rocky wanted some of that.

'Hey!'

Someone was leaning out of a bathroom window. A middle aged man, whose house had been festooned with red and yellow on Friday morning.

'Tell your brother he blew it,' his voice called after her.

Rocky scowled, thinking how fickle football fans were, then pushed on.

Was she going to have to put up with this all day? All week? Forever? Her brother didn't go down for a penalty. Her brother lost the cup. Her brother could have cost Melchester Rovers its future.

Rocky booted a stone across the road. It smashed against a wall on the other side.

She imagined Roy waking up whenever he did and finding he had a mirror on the back of his bedroom door. She envisaged him in his Melchester Rovers pyjamas, surprised to be staring back at himself. She hoped he'd take a good look and realise what he'd done.

Whatever.

It didn't matter.

The next time she saw him she would be in the Army.

Two days later, Rocky made her way to training. She had yet to see Roy since the cup final. That was because she was up before him in the morning and in the evenings she was busy, even eating her dinner in her room. She was one hundred per cent revising. There was a sign on her door saying DO NOT DISTURB.

Rocky liked being so in control.

And the truth was Roy was so down he'd not come searching for Rocky anyway. Mum had told her that he'd been shouted at from a couple of cars, people criticising him for not falling over and winning the penalty.

In fact, the only thing she would stop revising for was football. Tonight was the midweek training session. It was a cold night, frost already forming on the grass and pavements. So much for spring!

Sowerby trained on 4G now, so the weather didn't matter. And Rocky liked it cold. She always got so hot playing. She never felt the cold once she was over the line, on the pitch. Coach was right: it was different once you were over the line.

When she saw Ffion outside the dressing rooms she saw she wasn't in her kit, or tracksuit.

'Injured?' Rocky asked.

'Nothing much,' Ffion replied, touching her left calf. 'But just being careful.'

Rocky shrugged. She, herself, preferred to play through an injury. It was like she was telling her body not to be so pathetic, that she would decide when to stop. But she knew Ffion was different, sensitive to every twinge and pulse of her body. Rocky understood that – with the chance of a scholarship in America – she had a lot to lose. Then she wondered again. About Roy.

'Have you told him?' she asked.

Ffion shook her head. 'Maybe tonight. But I know he'd been getting all this grief and I feel like I should be comforting him, not making him feel worse. Is he coming?'

'Don't ask me.'

Ffion rolled her eyes. 'Are you still punishing him for not diving?'

'Is that what he said?' Rocky asked.

'Yeah.'

'Did he?'

'Yeah. He's sad about it. He knows you're avoiding him.'

'Right.' Rocky shrugged again. 'Well, he's

the one who blew it.'

'He needs your support, Rocky,' Ffion argued. 'Not your blame. You live your life your way and he puts up with you: why can't you let him live his life his way, with his outrageous fairness? It doesn't seem right.'

Rocky was stunned. So far she had been able to cope with feeling uneasy about not being there for her brother after his catastrophe. No-one had challenged her about it. Until now.

And now?

Now she was surprised to feel the sudden blow of shame. Why was she being so mean to her brother? So mean that Ffion had gone out of her way to criticise her.

ROCKY PLAYED HARD that night. The other players were used to it. Some days she could be brutal, flying into tackles, thrashing the ball at the keeper. They normally let her get on with it. As long as she didn't hurt anyone else.

Today she had no choice but to play so hard she didn't have time to think – or *feel* – anything.

As they trained, Rocky was aware of three figures on the touchline. She worked hard, trying to ignore them, but she couldn't avoid looking at her brother's posture. Had Ffion told him yet? How would he look when he was informed that the love of his life was moving thousands of miles away? How did people react to bad news?

Arms folded?

Head in hands?

Unrestrained sobbing?

Rocky wondered if he would drop to the floor like a puppet with its strings cut. But he'd not done that yet. This was all too much for Rocky. That shame Ffion had made her feel. And now a need to talk to her brother and say she understood why he did what he did, that she would have done it differently, but she was proud of him for staying true to who he was.

Urgh.

Rocky knew that the news from Ffion would finish him.

Then she was distracted by a surge of anger. Him. He was here. What the hell was Vic Guthrie doing at Sowerby training? And next to Roy? How was *that* okay?

Rocky hurled herself into her game all the more savagely. Trying to keep from behaving like a complete maniac, she gave it everything to mask her latest burst of anger.

But she knew she was running away from what she needed to do. The next stage of her taking control of her life. And that meant three conversations.

With Ffion.

With Vic.

With Roy.

They all had problems. Problems that affected Rocky.

Problems she wanted to resolve – or at least acknowledge.

Training finished, she went over to Ffion, who was encouraging some of the other players.

'You're right,' Rocky said.

'Am I?'

'Yes. I need to support my brother.'

Ffion nodded and tried, but failed, to smile.

'But only after you've told him about America.'

'Hmmm,' Ffion said.

'Go on,' Rocky said. 'Now.'

Ffion glared at Rocky, as if to say you can't order me around. But then she rolled her eyes.

'Okay,' she agreed. 'I will.'

'And while you're talking to my brother,' Rocky said, enjoying being so forthright, 'I'll talk to yours.'

'Vic?'

This was it. The first of three people she needed to talk to.

'Rocky?' Vic replied.

The floodlights were shrouded in swirling mist now. The kind of wispy low cloud that coils round lampposts and ghosts around on cold March evenings.

'I hear you're mad at your brother,' Vic said.

Rocky didn't like the look on Vic Guthrie's face. This wasn't going to help him. It was like he was happy that she and her brother were at odds. Why was it that people were always trying to tell her they knew what she was thinking? What did they know?

'No,' she said. 'He didn't go down. That's his choice. I'm not cross with him. I'm cross with someone else.'

'Ahh,' Vic Guthrie smiled again. 'Ffion's told you about leaving the country?' Then he whispered. 'She's not told Roy yet, you know.'

'I do know.'

'Right,' Vic smirked.

Rocky was sick of this. Vic was treating her like a child. He was taking her short answers like they meant she was shy. Whereas, in fact, she was cross. With him.

'I'm not mad at Ffion.'

Rocky saw Vic look over at Johnny Dexter.

'Why are you mad at Coach?'

Rocky laughed. Then she felt a surge of painful emotion. She had to fight hard not to cry by twisting her face, bearing her teeth. She lunged at Vic and hit him on the chest.

'You punched my brother. You punched him. You complete idiot. You bully. You… My God! I can't believe what you did. And I hate you for it.'

Vic Guthrie recoiled, staggering backwards because of the shock, not the force with which she had struck him.

'I know. I...'

'You pushed a referee over. You lost it. You lost it, Vic.'

'I'm sorry I hit Roy,' Vic said.

'No.' Rocky shook her head. Vic was shocked. She could tell that. But she was too. Shocked at what came out of her mouth, shock at how she had articulated her feelings so wildly. So aggressively.

'No what?' Vic looked panicked now. He was looking around him, aware dozens of eyes were on him. Dozens of eyes that had seen he had been pushed by Rocky.

'It's not about Roy. It's about me. I looked up to you. You were funny off the pitch and unrelenting on it. You were a tough in-control footballer. Then you lost it. Why did you lose it? It's done my head in.'

Vic swallowed. He was almost speechless, could only manage two words at a time.

'I don't...'

'Ever since I saw you hit my brother I've been feeling bad. Bad, Vic. I panic. I can't leave my room in the morning. And that's since you did what you did. Because now I get it that, if someone like you can lose it... if someone like you has problems... then someone like me can too.'

Still Vic didn't have much to say. Rocky was shocked that she'd managed to put into words the thing that had been worrying her for days. Now she understood it for herself, but she wasn't finished with Vic yet.

'And I know you don't know what to say,' she said, 'but I want you to say something. Now.'

ROCKY GLANCED OVER to see that Roy was sitting on a bench, Ffion next to him, grasping his hands. Roy was looking at his feet.

'She's told him, look,' Rocky said to Vic.

Vic Guthrie studied Roy and Ffion for a few seconds, then took a deep breath in. His face was pink. His eyes red.

'So… I've had a hard time,' Vic started. 'I lost something inside and I didn't know what to do. Then I went off the rails. All this and I was captain of a League One football team. It's crazy.'

'I know,' Rocky said.

'But it's getting better,' Vic went on.
'I've had... well... I'll tell you... I've had
counselling. Me. Mental health counselling!
And it's taught me something. Something
big. And I think you need to learn it too.'

'Why should I learn it? And from you?
After what you did?'

Vic smiled. But it was a smile that said
he was not so sure of himself. He wasn't
treating her like a child now.

'Well,' he said. 'You said you looked up to me.'

'I did.'

'I didn't know that. But I do now. And I take it seriously. And I am sorry, so very sorry. Dead seriously. I know that you can't talk to your dad like you used to. Can you?'

What was this? What was he saying?

Rocky felt like *she'd* been pushed now. She was winded. She wanted to run off and think about how she had no dad to talk to. Or mum. She didn't want to worry her mum. Vic had it spot on. She had no-one.

'So I want you to give me one more chance,' Vic continued. 'More as a friend.'

Rocky liked it that he had called her a friend. He was winning her round, after a bad start. He was actually starting to sound like an adult.

'Go on,' she said.

'Well… I realised I was isolating myself,' Vic confessed. 'I wasn't talking to anyone. And you need to talk. You need people to talk to, to listen to you. You have to talk to your mum, even if you think she has a lot on her plate. You have to talk to your brother: he's a good guy, too good, but, my God, he loves you.'

Rocky held back a sob.

'And you can talk to me. And to Johnny. You're not alone. Open up to people. It'll do them good to know you need them. I love it that Ffion needs me. I love it so much. But I didn't talk to anyone and I forgot all that and I lost it. My head was gone. But now I am coming back. If I can help you, Rocky…'

'I applied to join the Army,' Rocky confessed.

'What?'

'You're the first person I've told.' Rocky

stared at Vic's face. She knew he'd heard her. And she knew, too, that his reaction was everything to her. If he laughed or wagged his finger at her, she'd run off into the night and disappear.

'Oh my God,' Vic gasped, 'that is amazing. I can so see you in the Army, Rocky. It's perfect.'

'Really?'

'Oh yes. You'll smash it.'

Rocky screwed up her face. 'So I need to tell Mum and Dad?'

Vic nodded. 'You do. And Roy. But... can I ask...What about your football?'

'I'll still do that,' Rocky said.

'But...' Vic hesitated. 'You don't get it, do you? You're good.'

'Thanks.'

'No, I mean really good.'

Rocky shrugged.

'Did you see that woman with Johnny Dexter at your last game?'

Rocky remembered. Yes, her. The woman she was going to ask Coach about before she was concussed.

'Yeah.'

'She was a scout.'

'For Ffion.'

'No,' Vic laughed. 'For you. Coach and Ffion didn't want to tell you. They wanted you to be natural. But the scout liked you. I know that.'

Rocky couldn't stop herself grinning. A scout? For her?

But then the smile faded from her face. She saw, under a light, that Roy and Ffion were gesticulating at each other. Wild hand gestures. More trouble.

Ffion was walking, head down, hands to her face, in the direction of her car.

And Roy was running away towards the foot of the Moor. Rocky knew what she had to do. Forget about the scout. Again. And remember she was her brother's sister.

ROCKY WATCHED ROY running off on his own into the dark and swirling rain of the Melchester night. *What must be going through his head to run off like that?* she wondered. *Sprinting when he'd been stood in the cold. He'd never do that normally. It was an easy way of getting an injury.*

In her mind, she listed the things that might have made him run off like that.

The penalty stuff.

Her – his sister – blanking him after the cup final.

And all the other nonsense he'd had to put

up with over the last few months. Cleaver. Tynecaster. Dad. Mum. Her. It was endless.

And now Ffion telling him she was going to leave Melchester.

As Rocky saw him disappear into the night, she understood that she had never seen her big brother look so alone.

And so she went after him.

Up the canal. To the bus station. Then, when she reached the bottom of the Terrible 200, she saw her brother like a silhouette in the street lamps that rose up the hill with the steps. Roy slowed down the higher he climbed, so that when they both reached the top they were running side by side.

Rocky sat on the top step, gasping for breath, and looked down at the misty murky city.

Roy sat next to her. In silence. Rocky decided she would wait for Roy to tell her about his problems. In his own time.

'I applied to join the Army today,' Rocky told him after a pause.

'What?' Roy leaned back and stared at her.

'You heard me,' she smiled. She liked shocking him. She always had. Even when he was in the middle of a crisis.

'Right,' Roy mused. 'Are you sure about it?'

'Yeah,' Rocky said, desperate for the response from Roy that she'd had from Vic.

'Good, then,' Roy said at last. 'I can see you in the Army.'

'That's what Vic said.'

Roy didn't reply and Rocky wondered if she'd played it wrong. Was he still mad at Vic for punching him? Should she have kept her mouth shut?

'We've sorted it out,' Roy confirmed at last. 'Me and Vic.'

A cold wind came fluttering through the trees on the Moor behind them.

'You do what you feel most strongly you need to do, Rock,' Roy said. 'The rest will work itself out.'

'Thanks, brother,' Rocky whispered.

They sat quietly for what seemed like hours, although it was mere minutes.

'You know about Ffion too, then, I suppose?' said Roy, breaking the silence.

Rocky nodded, then put her arm round her brother's shoulder. She could feel him sobbing in the darkness.

'What do I do?' he asked her. 'I love Ffion. I don't want her to go to America. But...' Roy's speech broke up as he began to sob again.

'But you want her to do it too?' Rocky suggested.

'Yeah,' Roy sniffed. 'I want her to stay for me and to go for her. So what do I say to her about all that?'

Rocky sighed. 'Tell her what you just told me,' she said.

Roy laughed. Sort of. Then he stood up.

'Come on,' he said. 'Let's go home.'

They walked in silence across the Moor. At the top of their street they saw an old man walking his dog. The dog was called Rover; the man, Fred.

'Roy?' the man called out across the street.

'Fred. You okay?'

'I am, son.'

'I'm sorry about the Cup Final, Fred,' Roy said.

'Now you listen to me, young man. Stop that now. I am proud of you. You did the right thing. You are no diver. You never have been. And I suspect you never will be. You're a good lad. Be proud of what you did, whatever some of those idiots have been saying to you.'

'Thanks, Fred,' Roy called back.

'I'm sure that sister of yours agrees, eh lass?' Fred said, before turning to walk up his short garden path.

'I do, Fred,' Rocky said. 'I'm right behind him.'

Now she felt her brother's arm around her shoulder. And, for once, she didn't shrug it off.

Thank you

Big thanks to Simon Robinson for his ideas and enthusiasm for *Roy of the Rovers*. He is the Peter Taylor to my Brian Clough, except we have a better relationship. Also, to Lisa Henke, for her solutions to weaknesses in my game plan. Finally, to Rob Power, for editing all of my first six Roy books. Rob is being transferred to another children's book publisher, but it needs saying that, without him, Melchester Rovers would not be just a few wins from regaining Championship football for the first time since the 1980s.

YOUR REVIEWS MATTER!

Enjoy this book? Got something to say?
Leave a review on Amazon, GoodReads or with your
favourite bookseller and let the world know!